GREENLAND SAMPLE

S.I.S.M.O. ANIME BASED

DJS (YUVRAJ)

Contents

Foreword

<u>An anime novel by SISMO with three types of Manga style:-</u>

- Paperwork,
- Digital and,
- Greenscreen

Preface

Hi, umm. I'll keep this as *simple and short* as possible so I request you to keep up with me. So you are finally reading this means you've bought my work online or offline or just reading its free sample version (if you haven't pirated). Well,_ please pay all your little attention span for it is important and will end soon okay?_ While we talk about Anime a lot of us never force ourselves to promote it on a large scale or be part of the creator team who wants to make content similar to Japanese anime (at least that could match its level). But what you are reading is the result of the efforts, blood, sweat, and tears (literally) I put behind its making so that I could be part of that unknown community. Make content similar to the one we all love and can call our own!

Even if this series (consisting of 4 parts) turns out to be an unknown art I'll still be happy that I at least contribute some part by myself to the community of the few individuals who not only talk but put effort into creating what they say. Among the 3 Universes I've created, I've chosen the SISMO for the debut. Yes, I made 3 of them and they'll only come out if this book succeeds.

Rate my work or not; I don't care, but at least you can spread the word about this book for the sake of the *Indian Anime Community right?*

That's all I wanted to say and yes, I'll be sharing some dialogues like this in the upcoming parts of the book in this same 'Preface' section. (And you can skip the 'Prologue' section if you want).

Thanks for your patience SISMOs!

<u>Disclaimer</u>

This is a work of fiction. Names, characters, places, and incidents either are products of the author's imagination or are used fictitiously. Any resemblance to actual events, locales, or persons, living or dead, is entirely coincidental.

Please be patient while reading this copy for they are described as detailed as possible to help better understand with much easier language.

Thanks!

यह एक काल्पनकि कृति है। नाम, पात्र, स्थान और घटनाएँ या तो लेखक की कल्पना की उपज हैं या काल्पनकि रूप से उपयोग की गई हैं। वास्तवकि घटनाओं या स्थानों या जीवति या मृत व्यक्तियों से कोई

समानता पूरी तरह से संयोग है।

कृपया इस कॉपी को पढ़ते समय धैर्य रखें क्योंकि उन्हें बहुत आसान भाषा के साथ बेहतर समझ में मदद करने के लिए यथासंभव विस्तृत रूप से वर्णित किया गया है।

धन्यवाद!

これはフィクションの作品です。名前、登場人物、場所、出来事は、作者の想像の産物であるか、架空のものです。生死を問わず、実際の出来事、場所、または人物との類似性は、完全に偶然です。

彼らははるかに簡単な言葉でより良い理解を助けるためにできるだけ詳細に説明されているので、このコピーを読んでいる間、辛抱強くしてください。

感謝！

Acknowledgements

SPECIAL THANKS TO H.K. for Helping in the COMPLETION of the book.

पुस्तक को पूरा होने में मदद करने के लिए एचके के लिए विशिष धन्यवाद।

この本の完成にご協力いただいたH.K.に特に感謝します。

Prologue

In the unforgiving wilderness of Greenland, a bone-chilling wind howls across the icy tundra, carrying with it the whispers of a sinister past. A name once feared, a nemesis long thought defeated, rises from the shadows to exact an act of revenge so meticulously, that it's almost surgical. Meet **The Hunter**, a figure of enigma, unparalleled cunning, and icy determination.

In this gripping murder mystery, the past and present collide in a symphony of danger and intrigue. Hunter, the relentless arc enemy of a bygone era, emerges from the depths of obscurity, driven by a vengeance that knows no bounds. His reputation as a mastermind of malevolence precedes him, but his true intentions remain shrouded in an impenetrable veil of mystery.

As the chilling narrative unfolds, a group of former adversaries find themselves entangled in a web of fear and uncertainty. The stakes have never been higher as they race against time to decipher the hunter's cryptic agenda and survive his ruthless onslaught.

Set against the backdrop of Greenland's hauntingly beautiful yet perilous landscape, this story weaves a mesmerizing tapestry of suspense, betrayal, and redemption. Readers will be spellbound by the relentless pursuit of truth, the intricate layers of deception, and the unwavering resolve of both hero and villain.

Will the shadows of the past be vanquished once and for all, or will the hunter's icy grip tighten, leaving a trail of destruction in his wake? Prepare to embark on a heart-pounding journey into the heart of darkness, where survival hinges on deciphering the mind of the most dangerous adversary ever encountered. In this chilling tale, the line between justice and revenge blurs, and only the most cunning will emerge from the icy abyss unscathed.

CHAPTER ONE

But they don't know yet that Agapeta is dead. 19 December 2022, time, probably 6:00 in the morning, nobody knows anything but this innocuous fact: Agapeta was late for his breakfast.

"2 days ago," said Issaja.

Nukk;

"It was nearing the start of the school, everyone was on their way to the science period after filling their attendance except one. Not only did I dislike the period but I also hated the teacher the most. So, after scribbling my name on the attendance sheet with practiced precision, I slipped away. No one noticed as I veered off from the crowd, my heart racing with the thrill of rebellion. I found solace at the very back of the school, in the most secluded bathroom stall in Nuuk High—a place where even the janitor seemed to forget existed. Just then the principal announced through the loudspeaker- "LOCKDOWN! LOCKDOWN! This is an emergency alert. Please follow the lockdown procedures and shut all the doors and lights in the school tight. Rush to your nearest buildings."

To me, this was just another part of a mission if it just wasn't a drill. But since it was I did not pay any attention to the practice and waited. Just then seemingly all the lights of the building shut off all at once. It was a very cloudy and cold day. With the lights gone, it was close to the nighttime with no electricity. The bathroom went pitch black, this got me worried. *'Never did any drill cut off the building's lights like this...'*"

4 days ago,

Dubai;

Santoski mansion:-

Everyone was busy with their tasks when the realization hit hard that it had been a while since they last traveled together. After some discussion, they agreed to plan a holiday trip to a cold destination. Eventually, they settled on visiting Greenland, which happened to be Sara's hometown. This meant Sara would have the chance to reunite with her parents whom she hadn't seen in a long time, along with her brothers who lived there. They set a date for the trip in the upcoming week.

On December 15th, they boarded their private jet for a flight that lasted approximately 9 hours and 15 minutes, arriving in Greenland to face the extreme cold. Their faces turned red from the chilly weather. It was harsh those days. Sara then took her friends to her house in a nearby village. Sara's parents exuded kindness and hospitality. As they settled into Sara's house, they were greeted by the warmth of her family and the cozy atmosphere. It was a heartwarming reunion after a long time apart. Sara's parents were overjoyed to see her and her friends, welcoming them with open arms and a spread of delicious homemade meals. The warmth of family and friendship filled the air, making their holiday this year in Greenland truly special.

They were having such an amazing time there. Sleeping under congested beds with friends in warm clothes and blankets was tough to adjust to yet fun! Waking up in the cold mornings and washing clothes was a part of daily life. Hanging the freshly laundered garments on the outdoor clothesline, they watched as the faint tendrils of steam rose into the wintry air, a testament to the symbiotic dance between warmth and cold. They would also go on long walks in the evenings armed with steaming mugs of alcoholic coffee that promised to stave off the chill. The neighbors were also happy to see Sarah and some foreign guests in their village. They had planned to go to their luxurious lodge whose work was almost finished, the place at which they would spend the rest of their December of '22 after the farewell from the village. One night when Jumbo, Dominik, Hiroshi, Hannah, Randy, and Sarah were having fun together with casual conversations **they were unaware of the upcoming.**

(If these names seem alien to you then please consider reading The Trillionaire's Night Ride first. Getting familiar with our characters would promise to have an amazing effect on the ongoing story.)

LET'S CONTINUE:-

The next day (19 December 2022) arrived with bad news as when they woke up the Sismos were shocked by the brutal murder of a yak that resulted in the end of their warmth all of a sudden. Waiting for anything else to come up to something was futile! All the Sismo reached quickly at the scene. A deep slit in the neck of the dead was found in the neighborhood. Its blood flooded the snow floor seeming like a crimson carpet for the dead poor animal. The rest of the blood exiting the animal's body clothed due to the cold from ajar the slit. The most shocking thing was that someone (Obviously the killer) wrote 'ОХОТНИК ЗА СИСМО' (SISMO HUNTER) on the snow floor probably by using the same blood as the yak. The owners of the yak were in grief and crying. Both, the residents and the Sismos were shocked and scared because this happened for the first time in the village. Everyone in the neighborhood, including Sarah's parents was sent to Dom's cottage along with two Sismos (Pippo and 8) and with security. The Sismo had planned to leave for the cottage the same day but since the incident happened it has been canceled.

The holidays were already ruined by the mission upon now...

"One thing to remember is that Sarah's parents are also SISMOs."

Mains

SISMO BASED BOOK*Manga Included*

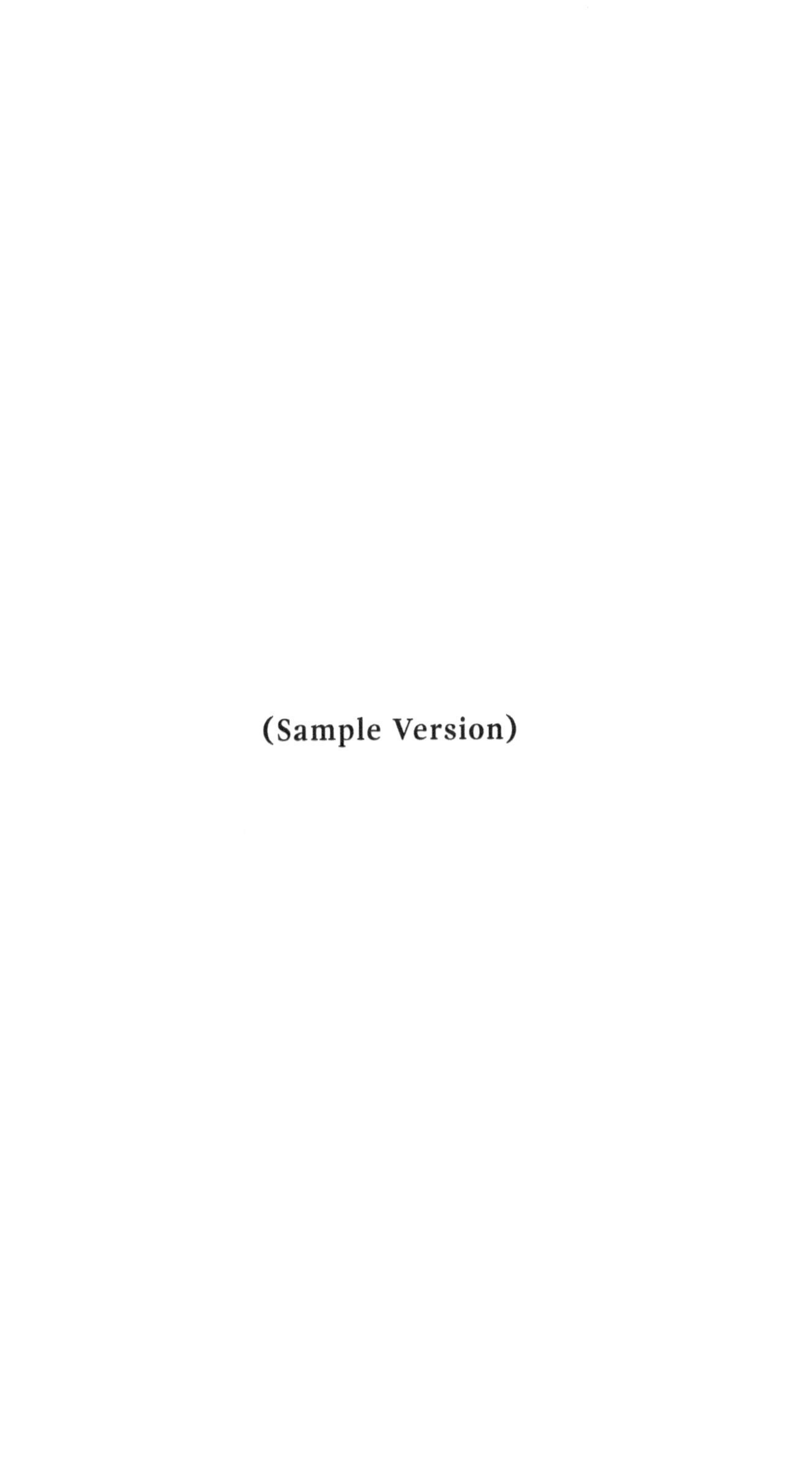

(Sample Version)

CHAPTER TWO

TADS

19 December 2022

11:32 PM

Finally, the long night comes when they have to remove the 'SISMO HUNTER' threat. Good thing that Somchai and Dominik understand Russian. The whole day has been dedicated to the plan for a capturing mission. They have long been brooding upon an effective plan to overcome the root cause of what happened in the morning. After experiencing, the harsh day and the bad reputation that the villagers now have for the community, they got only one chance to clean that impression on Sismo.

"Lights of the houses nearby must be on, all of them, to disguise the hunter that everybody's home." Said, Dom.

"I can't believe our holidays would be ruined in such a way!" Complaint Hiroshi in grief and stoked his forehead with his left palm revealing it against his brown bangs. That was the last thing they heard before jumping into the mission.

"Yeah, that would save more time and danger. Bro, we had come here to celebrate winter but it turned out into a mission."

'*True*' was what in everybody's mind to the statement and a feeling of grief, but none expressed or answered his obvious behavior as it would only demotivate them even further.

"Drop that chit-chat. Here's tonight's plan- We would be divided into four groups each of two members and a single person Judo for switching on the lights of only the close neighboring houses-" Said Sarah explaining the whole plan.

Little a while later they were into the action!

"Can't help that Somchai." Answered, Dom. "Some think that a Sismo is a bad person. Can't help it. At least for now.

Let's just clear the reputation and we'll continue what we were here for. Okay?"

"Hmm," Somchai switched on the last light on the upper floor of one of the far neighbor's houses. "All done!"

"Yeah? Alright. Let's move! Move!" They move out of the house from the small crack at the back side of the neighboring house they discovered earlier and cover it again with the wooden board. Both of them were just in the first neighboring that was three blocks away from Sarah's house. So they weren't really far away like the group of Sarah and Sylwia who were even a couple of houses further from them.

"I-I don't know if I would be able to make it..." Said Sylwia timidly.

"Huh, what?" Replied Sarah in an entirely different tone. "Why did you become a Sismo then? If you are scared just by looking at the blood in the morning, you have yet so much to learn girl. You're just a baby by this means and not any better."

Unruffledness is a Sismo's peculiar nature. Some have it more than the others.

"No. I am not scared; okay maybe a little. But it's very dangerous in the dark, especially in cold."

"So you're afraid of the dark?"

"I am not Dominik to be scared of the dark, the thing is I don't think I would be able to start something with such little experience. Plus we're all alone in the whole village now, and it's bugging me even more."

"Keep moving Sylwia, keep moving. Okay? No one's gonna feed you with their hand. You have to do it! Now that you've already chosen you must learn to be a Sismo before becoming an engineer! Just keep your mind harmonious while facing difficulties and you will make it. You quite followed me?!"

Sylwia nodded but didn't say a tad amid but swallowed hard... That was quite a motivation for now.

> "*Remember that when Sarah was born, no one could believe she was from Greenland. She was more like an albino because of her facial features and skin tone, including aqua-blue eyes, pale eyelids, and blond hair. She looks so much like a British nationality. Everyone in her village called her Angel because, to them, she looked like one.*"

"Now that everything's done let's move out."

Sylwia nodded again.

11:49 PM

"Heh-heh, glad to see you all okay! We finally made the first attempt successful and are here now!" Said the leader, Somchai Mcadams with a wide smile while his glasses reflected the room's light.

"Before starting, Hiroshi are you feeling okay now?" Asked Dominik

"Hiroshi fell from the chimney while we were sneaking in," Said Hannah looking at Hiroshi with concern. "I think he must have hurt his coccydynia."

"That's a quite large name for such a small bone you know," Hiroshi's voice easily expresses the pain he was in laying on the couch. He vailed in a low voice. "It makes it hurt even more.!."

"Don't worry son," Started Jumbo, Hiroshi's best friend. "Everything will be fine. Doctor's coming."

"You are my son you big piece of fat."

"No, you are, you stick man."

"You are!"

"No, you!"

"Hey! Hey! Hey! Are you over with?!" Randy exclaimed at them in his coarse voice. He's so fierce and a personal bodyguard of Dominik. At his voice, both Jumbo and Hiroshi stopped their conversation as they fear him.

"OOf, thanks, Randy." Said Sylwia stroking her forehead.

"Okay, listen." Started Dominik.

"I've already sent the photographs of the footprints at the scene to Andrew, and through the secret sources and to my surprise, the souls of the shoes, it came out to be of a very fancy company! Just like we buy (Like not that I buy them for myself but you may have). Sarah, I don't believe anyone from the village could be doing this right?"

"You can relax about that." She ensured.

> **"***Personal driver cum bodyguard; Andrew's in the cottage for the safety of all the villagers.***"**

"Now after that, we asked for a list of all the details of the villagers in this village locality who are at the family cottage right now. Just to be extra convinced we asked for photos of their shoes as well. And no one from them is of the hunter and that's proven now." Said Somchai.

That was a mood lifter for all of them.

"Yeah, he sent me the pictures." Randy showed the photos on his phone with a grin.

"But for once we-" Started Somchai but was interrupted by Dom.

"Yeah, at once-"

"... May I talk bro?"

"Fine, fine..." Dom was scared by Som's look. Sometimes Somchai McAdams is scary. No wonder he's known as the massacre in the *S.I.S.M.O. EYES community.*

"At first glance, the reports pointed out that 8 could be the killer because he has the same shoes and is of the same size as the photos. But it is highly impossible because he is a Sismo with us and doesn't have the guts to even be on a small mission yet."

"And he was with us all the time too," Said Jumbo.

"Yes. Plus Vaishnavi saw him sleepin' at that time so, yeah. But, according to the proofs, the design from the scene is also slightly, SLIGHTLY different from that of 8's product. That was a later finding this afternoon. No one could point a finger at one of us Sismos now. Bro, you may continue."

"Huh, no? I am cool. Go on."

"Bro, 8 doesn't have any idea that he was pointed to be the killer." Somchai chuckles.

"Unfortunately," Starts Judo. "I remember we have our parent's weapons, right Sarah? But..."

"Yeah. Kamas. But I am not sure where they are so we may not be able to use them."

Weapons for self-defense if posed in such a situation.

With that discussion, all of them went quiet for a while with sips of hot coffee. "Now, for this night we all have to stay up for the prevention of anything else that's unfortunate and that may happen." Said Sarah after a pause. Everybody exhaled in dejection since they couldn't do any better to express their grief.

"Still it's highly unlikely," Dom was against that flow of work. "If only we can catch him while he's closer to us."

"But we can't risk it."

"No worries, he won't come I know."

"How can you be so sure? Are you the one behind all of this? By that logic switching on the lights of the neighboring houses was a waste too." Sarah said in a rather grave tone this time.

"Don't be clumsy. I work in my own way."

"Dominik! Don't be so boasted!"

"Hey, don't shout!" Dom said in a grave tone too. "I know that'll be more effective. If you go by psychology then his showing himself today is more than impossible. And don't shout, tha-"

"But if he-!?"

"OKAY," Jumped Hannah in between them.

"Don't make a scene here!" Somchai shouted. "As a leader and I confirm that we'll go by the plans only. Bro, we understand that gut but we must not leave a single moment empty. Not a tad."

"Tch," Dom said closing his eyes and leaning back with both palms at the back of his head. "Do as you like. I'll save my energy for today... I would rather save every *tad* of energy I have."

Dominik sometimes can be so boasting of himself but no one can argue against it since his deductions and plans **never** fails.

They all were up for the rest of the time before morning but nothing happened on that stormy night.

"One thing to remember is that people of the village don't go out after 8:30 and sleep before 10:00. Moreover, they love their animals as their children so that was a deep black mark on Sismos name which must be cleaned at any cost. And salvation for them was only when they remove the threat from the village."

That same night at 12:23 AM

CALLING 8 WAS A HEADACHE

We didn't hurt a single wolf, even in self-defense!

21 December 2022

8:09 PM

All SISMOs are trained to be resilient. However, they may become weak at times while facing their personal phobias and fears.

"*Please be sure that 'Nighttime' in the novel follows the normal timeline of nighttime worldwide. Since Greenland experiences no night sky images are shown respectively darker for ease and elements follow the same as well.*

For example- The Sun during the nighttime would be called the Moon."

Just like Dominik deduced, the plan worked for two days. For two days there was no hunting or anything unnatural that happened. But staying up late at night was getting upon their nerves now. Though it seemed like a long time, most of it looked like a time waste not looking into clues and leftovers directed to the culprit. They have prepared many further plans for removing the threat in a more fastidious way! But with less sleep, they may not be able to execute the plan as sufficiently as the design itself sounds.

"I am quite sure who the culprit is. Still, taking his name would be haste for now."

"While it appears to be him we have to keep the possibility in mind that it might not be what we are thinking. If **he's** the killer and **theS.I.S.M.O. hunter**, then we have a first-hand advantage, since we already are a lot familiar with him. We just need some proof. Just one mistake by his side. Even a tad would do." Continued Somchai after Hannah.

He's the S.I.S.M.O. Hunter.

"He escaped the last time just because of his *duplicates* and because Alice trusted in him. But we are now ready for that, right Somchai bro?" Asked Hannah.

"We must first be sure that we aren't mistaking him to be **Reus** though." Dom interrupted in between.

"Yeah, I meant that only," Hannah replied to prevail. Just a sweet nature that Hannah has.

"*One thing to remember is that Hannah may show interest in morbid things because of her personality. She's more than fine with blood and gore. But don't think that makes her a villain. "*

"Hmmm... Right cousin." Somchai closes his eyes and falls into deep consciousness with a sunk head and all his finger joints. Everybody was in the house's small drawing room while the villagers were still in the luxurious cottage. After deciding the next move for quite a while with the four **#horsemen_of_Sismo** a.k.a. Somchai, Dominik, Hannah, and Sarah, the final decision was that patrolling at night was indeed the safer option for now. As they already knew or suspected, who the killer might be, about whom they were more than sure than its opposite, they were sure to go by this plan. He was surely very adamant about changing his habits. That was their main weapon. However, staying up for even one night straight was not a piece of cake; and now it was the turn of the third time.

"So, it's decided," Starts Somchai; waking from his meditation. (His friends thought him to be asleep) "Staying up for the patrolling is indeed a safer and the best option at the same time! To keep things fastidious, we've devised a plan to do it on alternative days. (He reveals the plan he made with the eye bosses at early dates) Now I know that it would be hard for you but, Akira, Sarah, Sylwia, and Dominik will be patrolling for today's night-" He just repeated the whole discussion in a crux.

"The rest of the names will do it tomorrow." Finishes Dominik on Som's behalf.

"な, なに!?... 今日のために...? (What!?... For today?)" Akira's reluctance could be clearly seen.

"Yes. See, you can't forbid, Akira..." Says Hannah. "That's the best that we've observed from all of you. Sarah usually studies very late at night, Sylwia does too; *I have to become an engineer* (Said Sylwia slowly in the background)

Dominik consumes coffee; *Hey, don't put it that way. I have to work...* (Said Dominik in the background) and for you, I think for your internship you've also worked overtime, didn't you? Akira?"

"H-は... (yes)" Still reluctant.

Forbid? What's this monstrous word now?

"So you can do it. You just have to."

"Hannah won't be able to make it today because she's a sound sleeper." Sarah taunts Hannah and chuckles.

'Staying for patrolling, you can do it Sylwia.' Sylwia *motivates herself meanwhile with a scared and shaky voice.* *'You can do it. Remember you are a SISMO. You've already fought once, maybe twice. You've also witnessed and worked in the Reaper case. Focus baby, focus.'*

"No. I mean, you would be the only boy with all the girls." Said Akira to Dom; interrupting Sylwia's affirmations and she jumped in shock.

"So?"

"What if some girl looks at you with dirty eyes? *What the...!* (said Sarah and Sylwia in unison)"

"Huh? You see me with lusty eyes?"

"いいえ、兄弟。しかし、他の人にとっては- (No. But for the other-)" Sarah and Sylwia pulled Akira and started beating her with their kicks.

"Well. Judo would also be joining so I won't be the only one." Dominik said nonchalantly with folded hands.

8:16 PM

As per the plan, all the members would be dispersed in all directions of the house. North-South_West-east→ Dominik, Akira, Sylwia, and Sarah. This design has been executed from the start of 8:00 in the afternoon. The plan was simple to follow- the same code of conduct that was being followed for the last two days. They have to look out for anything unnatural and inform everybody connected through the Bluetooth speakers on the ground.

Akira

was looking at the condensed smoke-like vapor from her mouth till it disappeared in the cold air.

(Initially, Akira's weren't working so Randy had to fix them before performing his own contribution to the plan)

" 物が見えない... (I can't see a thing outside). Thankfully I've brought my binoculars while packing after Hannah called." A quasi smile passed Akira's face and she put the binoculars on her eyes, sitting on the kitchen slab, looking outside the window with dark, black, Sorbus groenlandica or Greenland mountain ash.

"木木木. 森森森, (Trees, trees, trees. Forest, forest, forest.)" Said Akira looking at the outside scene. "ただの暗い森...怖い暗い森... (Just dark forest... Scary dark forest...)"
For instance, there was nothing to see on that cold night.

Meanwhile- Sarah and Sylwia;

Sarah and Sylwia were sitting across in the same room, hall, peeking out through the closed windows on both sides. While Sylwia was shivering out of the extreme that night, cold Sarah on the other hand stood like a stone with a fixed view outside the mirror. She was more than focused. Not like a statue, but she was a much older SISMO than Sylwia so she simply doesn't feel the same challenges with weather conditions as a normal man would feel. Sarah started in 2011 during which she faced numerous cases related to all that the world could suffer because of and gained experience in all kinds of turmoils on the other hand, Sylwia joined in 2017, and soon after, in a couple of years, she moved to Dubai for the 2019 new year party after which a pandemic started and they lived there ever since. Dubai was less prone to crimes. Sylwia couldn't gain much experience there. Though she was called upon for the Reaper case ? DEAD BITE BY SISMO, the case still didn't give her much confidence, other than seeing death threats and some dead bodies. Common. There was but one exception in Dubai ? *THAT NIGHT BY SISMO*, but other than the mujrim case there had been no serious cases, at least for her. Moreover, *she wasn't in the mujrim case in the first place!* Anyway coming back,

Sarah's focus started to notice that Sylwia was shivering sitting on the sofa through the reflection of the glass. "Still scared?" She seemed to have asked loudly and Sylwia jumped in her place with a heart-pumping shock.

Mini heart attack.

"N-No. I was just freezing..." She turned back her head and answered.

"Are you sure..?"

"Y-Yeah."

"Look, if you are scared then just take it as a mathematics topic," Sarah finally turned her head back at her as she spoke and to its initial afterward.

"Huh?" Sylwia couldn't get it.

"In engineering, maths is much easier than physics, isn't it? You are not afraid of your mathematics book are you?"

"Mathematics book? But what changes does that make anyway."

"KEEP LOOKING AT THE FOREST! (Sylwia moves her head back toward the forest as well obeying Sarah's suggestion) I am telling you that you are in a much safer position than Akira alone in the kitchen right now. You're studying to become an engineer right? Then it's simple-Take the kitchen as the Physics room, Akira's alone in there with physics so it is much harder(riskier) while you are in the mathematics room because you are not alone (you are with me right now). Does that make it simpler for you now?"

"Well, Sarah, that explanation was simply so absurd you realized that?" Sylwia stifled and laughed at it.

"I am a Soldier, not a diplomat! Cut to the chaise!!"

"Well, yeah. I can understand your expression on it but I am not-"

"Listen to this- Hatchling sea turtles emerge from their nests, scramble down the beach, and swim off into the open sea, where they feed and grow. Even at their hatching, they are prone to becoming some vulture's meal. You know that? (Sylwia nods in silence; it was better to remain silent right now because Sarah was speaking) The thing is that these baby turtles have only one goal at the time they are born. I don't think they have any idea that they may die while going to the sea. Such dedication is not lacking in humans though. But a human as a SISMO does not feel the same emotion of fear related to it. A baby turtle may not be able to save himself but *even if you're weak you'll somehow find a way out.* That's why there exists a death threat but the chances of death of a SISMO other than aging are very minimal. No fear, still some precautions kill the probability of losing and the brain works faster at the time. Don't worry lil girl. I am with you to guide you in every way possible. Be the sea turtle who is not afraid of death, just go to the sea. I have your back." She finishes.

"T-Thanks... Um. But, I am not scared but just freezing..." She continues.

Sarah turns her head slowly at Sylwia again with a blank expression by wide eyes.

"T-Thanks for the motivation, by the way..." Sylwia says sarcastically.

Dominik and Randy;

They were sitting in the dark attic by the small window through which only the moonlight was coming in on that cold night and the rest of the place was covered in dark shadows. The thing they didn't share was that Dominik was looking at the north part of the house with the drone camera while sitting away from the northern side in the attic while Randy was looking out of the same window (which was the eastern side). But the dusty wooden floor they were sitting upon and the talks between them were mutually shared.

"I just forgot that an eye must be kept from the upper part as well." Says Dominik while looking at the live footage from his drone on his phone.

"I didn't know that the man whose animal crocked is blaming 8 because he misunderstood him to be the only Sismo there at the lodge. His neighbors and known ones were calming him continuously. He even attacked me! I just went there to see if someone needed something but seeing the man's furious behavior towards 8 and at me, I could say that the old bastard is insane right now. It's better to keep our distance from him right now." Replied Randy about his visit, sitting with one hand on his right knee while the other pressed at the back for support.

"You shouldn't say that Randy," Dom said. "People of this village love their animals as their very children."

"Yes, sir. You are not at objection at that," Randy replied.

"It is natural to show such behavior to the person he thinks is the reason for all cause." Dom continued.

"Yes sir."

"You came with Andrew?" Dom asked after a pause, changing the topic.

"Yes sir. He drove me here. Paige and Abayomi were also with me in the car while dropping."

"Nice that you took all the precautions. You are so adamant at times. Now I just hope that Judo would also come home safe and sound."

"Judo's out too?"

"To sit at the retail shop, yes."

"It's just like the recent pandemic Dominik... uh., SIR," Randy said. "We must take precautions to be on the safer side while we're out."

Dominik chuckles at the observation. "Yes, it is." He says afterward.

"Did the villagers in the lodge yearn for something? I mean other than to switch to their previous environment?" Dom started after a little longer pause this time.

"Not really Dominik, uh...SIR."

"About 8, Vaishnavi, and all?"

"They're doing fine as well. Several bodyguards are at the line for security as well."

"Right..."

"But sir, I don't suppose Reus may know about the lodge. I mean it is far away from where we are. It is near the city. Plus it is our owned million-dollar lodge. In this light security seems useless."

"You are not at objection either, Randy," Dom had his right index finger resting on his lips. "But *the more you show yourself the more you are prone to death.* This SISMO saying has a much wider aspect in real life too than just being among the Sismos or being one of the Sismo yourself... Celebrities are, at times, at more risk than normal men. Why would you think we spend so much on bodyguards and high security? Plus we can't stop the news from spreading either. Even if our single hair moves from our heads. In a millisecond it becomes a brooding thing and news headlines. In this light, Randy, security is rather a critical topic."

Randy in reaction nodded and swallowed heavily, remaining silent.

"Gussing that the wind would not go harsh tonight?"

"Yes. If we believe the internet..."

"By the way how's Hiroshi doin'? How's his ass..?" He asks and starts a mediocre laugh.

"Randy..." Dom says intensely and gives him a serious glance.

"S-Sorry sir."

"Remember you are a bodyguard right now... Have control of your language. As for him, he's doing fine. We called the only doctor from this village this afternoon while you were at the lodge. She said he'll be fine if he rests properly in a couple of days." He was rather solemn this time.

"Local doctor? Well, that's fine."

"She works in the city. She was here for a visit to meet her village relatives."

"Oh... Much better then. Her visit is like Sarah's as well." With that reply, the place again broke into silence while they both started the monitoring more seriously.

Akira;

"おい何?!! (Wait what?!!)" She seems to have seen something after some time. She focuses the lens more on the weird dark figure hiding among the dark trees. A silhouette. "ちょっと待って何？(Hey, wait what?)" It was a man, a teen, with just a thin jacket with fur and skinny jeans. So underdressed for the cold climate in minus. SO WEIRD...

Since, because of the midnight and the quiet distance, it was impossible to recognize the dark-appearing entity in the distance. Not only that, but his movements seemed weird and noticeable as well. That was quite alarming to look at!

Akira was alarmed!

She calls upon them and in a second everybody's Bluetooth gets connected. All the calls connect simultaneously, i.e. Sarah, Sylwia, and Dominik. She informs that there seems to be some strange figure at a distance from the house peeking back and forth in an eerie way! She tried her best to explain his outfit and that seemingly his attention was on the house- "H-how do I explain this? It's moving in a very weird manner. Wait, now it stopped! It's moving again?!" Akira was trembling as she spoke. She didn't know the exact words to express her feelings. It was then she felt her heart pumping so fast that it would jump off her chest and felt sweat dripping from her head *even at that extreme temperature.*

"Don't worry Akira, we are coming!"

"Just don't move your focus from the thing! We'll be in no time there! Over and out!!" Commanded Dominik after Sarah finished followed by a ti-tii.

"*FOCUS?* それはどういう意味だと思いますか？　（What does that suppose to mean?)" Akira can't understand plenty of that language.

All she's interested in are Shoguns, carrots, and lip balms.

"Where is it, Akira?!" Sarah was the first to approach the kitchen followed by Sylwia and then both the boys.

She moved her finger in a hurry and behind the dust of snow with a blow of cold wind in the distance they saw the figure. They overwhelmingly confirmed that it really seemed familiar. Like they've already had a memory of someone from the past they knew of the very outfit. **Reus.**

As they saw him all the expressions of the Sismos changed from shock to an intense one, even of Sylwia who was being the most fragile mentally to the unknown danger.

Randy- "Do we need any other proof?"

Dominik- "Doesn't look like. That's a clear sign. Over 90 %."

Sarah- "He'll pay for the animal's death..." That statement reflected haterade.

All of them continued their expressions in their tone as well.

Akira- "もう逃げられない... (He'll have no escape now...)" She takes out her katana from her big traveling bag that she kept on her right side on the slab to have snacks late at night. "Look, I've brought my すごいkatana as well to slice him!" The ending of her statement was rather with eye smiles.

"Keep moving!" All of them rush into a sudden marathon and Dom commands them with the words. Akira hesitates as she is still sitting on the slab. With a low enthusiasm but deep exhale she jogged after them.

"We don't have time! Keep movin' your asses!!!"

"Randy!!!"

"Sorry, sir..."

"Zuzanna, stay at home and take care of its safety...!"

"What? But it is a great opportunity for me..!" She was shocked by hearing that from Dom's side.

"Just do as I say...!" All of the SISMOs rushed out through the front door that opened with a thud while Sylwia stopped by it, following them with her eyes helplessly. As their footsteps died and they disappeared cold wind rushed inside the door. Sylwia covered her mouth with the collar and with resentment. Because she was lacking the first mission experience she went to the door knob and as the door was about to be closed to the fullest she saw a Mavic

2 pro resting upon an upright wooden barrel outside. Covered with snow the indicator lights were on showing that it was calibrated and in fact, the camera was working too.

Footsteps rushed straight to the point where they saw Reus beside the frontmost three snow-covered mountain ash trees. He wasn't present there anymore. Smoke-like vapor coming out of their mouth was hindering their way of view while running but they were outsmarting in with their fast foot speeds. "Randy! Pass a gun at me..."

"Sir!" He tossed a gun in the air and Dom caught it and unlocked it.

"Knew you were keeping two of the same weapon." Dom continued while running.

"I have a few other weapons as well," Randy commented back to him. "That's what I've learned at the ghostly mountains." He finished with a smirk. They were increasing their speeds as their destination was getting reduced with each air-cutting step. Cold air passed their faces decreasing the temperature and numbness of the exposed skin. Paled.

"Keep silent!" Akira orders and coughs. They finally rest their feet at the location where Akira coughs even more with her pallor hands on her chest while Sarah is stroking her from behind.

"Akira,"

"それは大丈夫。私はfine,(It's okay. I am fine,)" Akira cleared her neck. "Get into hiding..."

"Hiding?"

"Yeah..."

"But why hiding?" Randy asked.

"What are we supposed to be doing here?" Akira replied as she finally got her hands off her chest.

"Randy," Sarah broke into their conversation. "She must be telling us to retreat behind the trees."

"What?" Randy gets it. "O-Okay..."

"Akira is naive in English. Told you."

"In position!" At Dom's order, they hide behind the snowy trees in bumpy but straightforward directions focused on the dark abyss inside of the forest. They all were intimidatingly looking at the darkness.

Both Randy and Dominik get into positions, Randy unlocks his gun, active to fire. Akira draws her katana from the 鞘 (Saya or scabbard) while Sarah is bare-handedly looking directly inside the dark forest after the footrest. There was complete dead silence not even the air was bothering it. Some time had already passed but there were no movements as earlier.

As some guy moving back and forth.

"I am sure I saw him here..." Akira tries to persuade without anyone even asking her to.

She was making them believe that her eyes mixed with the equipment of binoculars couldn't lie so easily.

She was sure of the location they were in as well.

"Sarah," Randy whispers in the middle of his waiting. "Where's your weapon? I have some pocket knives. Grimy but shall I pass it to you?"

"I don't need no weapon to kick *your* butt. So what's this loser Reus anyway?" She replied intimidatingly staring at the forest.

"What?" Randy said slowly to himself. "Hey! Stop being nasty for the mistake I haven't been involved in..."

"Oi... Stop... That was too noisy." Dominik intimidatingly told them to focus on the current situation right now.

"Sir but... Hump alright." What could have Randy said? There was no other statement that he could have been in his favor that he could agree to. Sarah didn't reply either.

Some minutes had passed again. The cold wind started to bother the silence a bit. And as per the training they were now supposed to kick into some finicky action quickly.

"Follow the darkness and retreat behind the trees again as and when I signal with my hand," Dominik said slowly, going deeper into the cold dark woods.

"He was right at this spot we are on which right now..." Gestilated Akira.

Footsteps felt like they were walking on the wet sand. After getting inside, when the exit was left far behind into the much darker atmosphere of the forest, Dom raised his right hand horizontally to his body pointing to the right with all his fingers. *Signal* to retreat!

They were in active positions ready for the unknown **danger.** In a couple of silent seconds, Sarah's eyes widened with what she realized about the place they were in as they heard a unison of howls echoing from the inside in all directions, Sarah revealed that sometimes, she realized right now, there were wolves to be seen at night! Nocturnal, dangerous, and in a bunch.

"..."

There were no replies to that shock but rather stares of wonder that each passed to the other.

"Don't worry you, Sarah," Says Akira. "Once I fought a lion. I will crush whatever is making that sound!!" Her enthusiasm didn't seem congruous with the following mission. The deep forest was turning into a haunting place now.

Dom signals again and rubbing away the resistance of fear they jogged into much deeper woods and hid behind one of the trunks of the deeper barks. The air was getting rough but ironically wet at the same time, there were flakes of snow falling on their heads. The mutual was that both of the observed types were equally harsh. So extremely cold that they had to cover their noses the stop the flakes from entering their noses which would otherwise be harmful to the body.

"Know that the coldest the universe can get is up to -273.15 degrees Celsius only," Says Sarah rubbing off the snow from her head while the other hand was covering her mouth and nose. "That is -459.67 degrees Fahrenheit?"

Sylwia on the other hand was putting the pieces together in her mind.

Why do they want to keep her at the house while everyone's out?

Why was the Mavic paired?

And why was it kept outside?

Was it our equipment?

She was still observing the drone sitting inside, still keeping herself close to the entrance gate when she felt the hunch to check the attic part of the house. Only Dominik is so interested in the drones that he would use them in every minimum and harsh way possible to gain their pleasure and explore their uses in every condition.

"Since he is the most interested, and, in the attic, he was with Randy some moments ago. I gotta check out the part anyway. I must!" She said to herself.

Wolves! There were plenty! Not to be seen with the eyes yet, but there was a huge pact and that was confirmed, whose simultaneous (not quiet) howls were filling the dark forest with wetlands. As they, fearlessly, step ahead the howling promoted to barkings and growls. Like it was a clear warning not to come face-to-face with them.

Doesn't look good.

"Are they aware of our presence?" Randy forces the possibility.

"The Greenland wolf is a subspecies of gray wolf that is native to Greenland," Sarah starts her lecture on her knowledge about her home country. "Historically, it was heavily persecuted, but today it is fully protected and about 90% of the wolf's range falls within the boundaries of the Northeast Greenland National Park. Looks like these are the 10% of the left. Scientific name: Canis lupus Orion:-

- Arctic wolves communicate via sounds and the position of their tail.
- The Arctic wolf is smaller than the gray wolf.
- Arctic wolves tolerate complete darkness.
- Arctic wolves live in packs of 5 to 7.
- Only the leaders of the pack mate-"

"**What I asked,** is that are they,..aware of our presence..?" Randy controls his anger at Sarah's lecture on wolves.

"As I said, they tolerate complete darkness. *Animals active at night are called nocturnal.* That directly means we might be in danger. Not sure if they recognize a human intruder in their area yet or not." She replied unruffled.

"That's the only thing that keeps us from being confident. These animals can hunt during the day but are more successful at night," Dominik says. "When wolves are active at night, *they typically chase prey.* Wolves are also highly adaptable, changing their daily activities according to when their prey is active. **During the winter, a pack will commence hunting in the twilight** or early evening and will hunt all night. Sometimes they travel tens of kilometers as well and in our condition, I can only assume that they are getting ready for that very action." He said while walking ahead with everyone.

"私はあなたが今言ったことのどれも理解できませんでした. (I didn't get any of what you said right now.)" Akira said in a low tone after a pause. Disoriented mentally.

"That means we certainly *are* in great danger! Isn't Reus himself in danger as well by that fact?" Randy focused on the essence of the whole matter ignoring Akira.

"Just keep moving! What are Sismos without any adventure in our lives?" Sarah was so confident her smirk came unavoidably.

"Thanks for that useless knowledge..." Randy replied after a pause disparaging the SISMO traits.

"Our lives are filled with complications anyway." Dom moved forward with much seriousness.

"Don't worry Randy we are Sismos so we'll be fine." Akira broke into the conversation.

"Are Sismos really that resilient to death conditions?"

Dominik and Sarah didn't reply to that question.

"W-wait... What does that suppose to mean," Randy hesitated at their silence.

"Let's face whatever comes to our side. If we are well trained then nothing will take our lives away." Sarah made a heroic statement in between the howls of the wolves in unison staring back at Randy. Dominik raised his hand in the same manner. That was clearly the sign to move ahead.

"The only danger here is us!" Sarah moves ahead fearlessly as she leads.

"B-but..."

"Don't worry Randy," Akira started in her thin, unflipped yet baby-like voice. "I've fought a lion and won the victory against him. We will crush them!" The last line of her speech was exaggeratedly coarse. Still, that was cute.

After quite some time their route was blocked by a giant fallen pile of trunks of the Mountain ash trees and the cherry on top to block their visions was fulfilled by the snow that was covering most of the part of its black trunk from the upper part horizontally. That was quite high, to be honest. All of them were of decent height.

Akira was the least among them standing at a height of 5'7.

Dominik was 6'0.

Sarah at 5'8 and Randy at 5'10. But that wasn't still enough.

They clutched upon it, tried to see the world beyond somehow but all was in vain hopes. Futile nature. Their hands were wearing off the snow covering the trunks. Even if they removed it there was a potential chance of getting their gloves toured with giant holes on it gifted by the roughness of the black trunk's texture. Sarah but being professional in climbing from childhood managed to climb upon it somehow. Giving a hand to Dominik they climbed most of the part while, though it was very hard to bear the weight of the clothes, Akira climbed upon Randy's shoulders to see what was beyond this heavy pile of trunks. It looked like they were tiny people with some titan trees. How were the trees so big anyway!?

Never mind, all three of them i.e. Sarah, Akira, and Dominik peeked from behind the trunks, and what they saw shocked them! Akira was more than amused, and rather than being concerned, she felt a sense of relief and satisfaction to see Reus sitting upon the snow with wolves surrounding him with a little moonlight while he was petting one of them with his left hand. He was wearing the same fur coat with skinny black jeans as three years ago. His black stylish glasses rested upon his head supported by the back of his ears and his hair was silky, shiny, long, straight, and pitch black in color. He also had the same black mask on his face as before. He looked a bit undressed for the extreme temperature but the main thing being that he was actually, physically present there in front of their eyes after three years was more amusing!!!

And that was somewhat nostalgic too since he was an old enemy.

Akira- "Look, I was always right."

Dom- "Is he for real?"

Sarah- "Yes he is... He's *petting* the wolves..!?"

Akira- "I can't believe this he's still after us."

Beneath them, Randy, for support, was putting the whole of his pressure pressing the trunks while Akira, his sister, was standing upon him. His face perfectly reflected the pressure he was bearing at that moment. His eyes were tightly closed as well. Though he was a bodyguard of Dominik that doesn't mean he could bear the amount of weight he was bearing at present. Neither he could do it with the SISMO training right now.

"A-are you all done for..?" He asks with the reflections of his feelings through the medium of words. But his voice couldn't reach them since that was too suppressed. Randy dismayed in the middle of this observes some little footsteps from his left. Suddenly he hears the heavy barkings of one of the wolves that come to his ears from the same side. A wolf! That catches the attention of all three Sismos as well. Reus was attracted and followed the barks with all the wolves he was petting. In a moment that turned to be an ambush of wolves from all directions. As the four of them realize that they were trapped Dominik returns his vision with a shock and sees no one sitting upon the snow ground lighted by the moon anymore. Akira jumps off lifting her weight from Randy's shoulders and does a tactical roll upon the snow and the rest of them start towards the danger that they were already prepared for. Akira raises her *katana*, ready to fight but there was a bunch they couldn't take down in the darkness, as she realized. Dominik shoots on the ground unruffled.

Sarah- "Hey! Don't try to hurt the native animals! They are rear!!"

Dom- "I am not aiming my bullet at them, just trying to scare them off! Understand that!" His eyes suddenly reflected unruffled nature.

Akira swung her sword and used her *kenjutsu* techniques to keep them away from attacking but the wolves were very angry, with fierce eyes, and the energy by which they were trying to bite, repeatedly, was much of a terror. They were biting the air with their fangs to get a part of the Sismo's body somehow to reduce to tatters and cut into slivers the pure prey for the day..!

While the SISMOs were struggling to find the exit, which seemed like a distant dot of light from their standing location, the darkness was advancing for the wolves. Randy too was scaring them off with his bullets somehow but at the moment it was becoming emptier bullet by bullet as well.

Randy- "Can't we run!?"

Dominik- "You can't outsmart the speed of the wolves can you Randy!?" He replied in the middle of his shooting. Just in some moments, the wolves retreated, hiding behind the trees again. That made the surroundings as shocking and silent as death. The situation was, as they realized turned so deadly that they couldn't afford to risk their lives anymore. The air smelled like burning fire and gunpowder and the beast's terror was more than enough for being a good reason to get the hell out of there.

DID THE WOLVES '*TACTICALLY* RETREAT'?

"Как давно это было? Такое ощущение, что навсегда..! (How long has it been? Feels like forever..!)"

A voice emerged in the silence of the night.

"Здравствуйте... Кажется, вы уже разобрались с моим грандиозным выходом. (Hello... Seems like you've already figured out about my grand entry.)" Continued the cold, sexy, and somewhat coarse voice echoing from the middle branch of one of the surrounding snow-covered trees.

This was **Reus.** The Sismos figured it out as they turned to follow the voice's direction. He was hanging upside down like a bat with a leather zip tie, looking like some ninja equipment, tied to one of the branches, and with long black hair hanging down. His hands were closed, glasses were on and his contrast with the moonlight looked epic, to be honest. The moonlight carved the shape of the left side of his body.

They were, the SISMOs, not shocked at seeing him but still couldn't say a word only intense expressions on their faces...

"Не хочешь сказать ни слова? Ну, если ты не понимаешь моих слов, Услышь это сейчас, the last count of our meeting still is yearning for its sequel. (Don't you want to say a word? Well, if you can't understand me, hear this now, the last count of our meeting still is yearning for its sequel.)" He continued.

"Believe me, it ain't gonna be so fruitful. At least for you..." His voice turned intense. Saving himself from Dom's bullet he landed on the ground.

'WHAT..!?'

That was quite a big shock to him, and everyone. Dom couldn't lose it easily when he pulled his trigger against a target. That's not quite the case that he'll ever lose while shooting. It's like the dark in the light.

Quietly exaggerated.

But it's really like this...

'D-Damn it..!'

"Long time no see the *S.I.S.M.O. HUNTER... You killed-*" Sarah was evenly grave at him.

"You didn't answer... Liked my grand entry?" He spread his arms showing off, trying to look cool, and walked a few steps towards them and stood a meter away.

"Amazing huh? Just like me... Me talking to you is quite ironic you know that? Мы русские (We Russians), you know what we have the commonly saying words for people like you? We have a good saying-"

"We are agents, not diplomates! Cut to the chase!" Randy said.

"Преступники..! (Criminals)" Reus continues in Russian.

"What the-" Randy was getting frustrated. "You Russian head still speaking in that language! You killed the animal for making contact with us, haven't you? Just to make contact, that's sick!"

"Who arc you anyway?! A new S.I.S.M.O. I am guessing." He was so stern at him.

"You forgot me! How!? I kicked your butt years ago! Don't joke around!!" Randy was frustrated.

"Greetings... Always happy to see a new face."

Stubbornness and sophistication (or complicated is better) were always a nature subconsciously set in him.

To Reus, he's always flamboyant and right in whatever he does. An extremist.

"You killed..." Sarah said to herself. Her voice was shaky.

"That kill... Yeah, sad for some," He was so nonchalant and overconfident. "But that grief is nothing compared to millions of those who suffer the same because of you Sismos. You all are criminals! You Sismos quite make it look really a nice type of a deed you do, but it's not all things like that! You simply are criminals, killing people! Hiding your cruelty behind the fact that they were criminals after all, but killing ultimately is a crime. When you put the man's family in grief, then you are a criminal to the same extent. And you keep doing this again and again. But someone needs to stop that overflowing. Someone... That someone should be, has to be **me** after all. If that ideology makes me a *Hunter.* Then that's what I am."

There spread a moment of silence that moment broken only by the sound of the wind.

The S.I.S.M.O.s were on one side while Reus was alone on the other. Facing each other. Plainly.

"...The animal." Sarah finally finished her statement to herself, filling the silence around

"I..," Dom started after a pause with a very calm tone. "Don't wanna revise out loud *all ideologies* and traits of a Sismos repeatedly to...(exhale normally) idiots like you... I've already done it thousands of times. Save that but there must be a reason why the government supports that ideology. Mend the ways of the government if you are against us then... In that case, to save-"

"Killing is a crime huh? You seem to have a great understanding of this field. You understood what killing is about quite well then," Sarah interrupted in the middle. Dom was a bit annoyed by it but it's okay. "Then why did you... kill the poor animal who had nothing to do in this matter?! Humans do morbid stuff, no doubt, but domestic animals don't even bother to do a tad right? Then why did *you* kill and become a murderer like us? Even if it was a necessary source to start our communication with, you could have killed one of us S.I.S.M.O.s instead! Why wasn't it like that in the first place? We are Sismos with our lives on the line! If removing us *threats* is your only motive then you should have done it with someone who was one of the parts of that threat! If it was one of us then it could have been justified! The way you choose to start this, in this way, sadistic offense! You are a criminal on both sides! For Sismo believers and non-believers! Do you realize? You have a good sense for murder and now *you are a criminal as much as we are by that logic. Even bigger!! Am I wrong, Reus?!*"

Her voice was even more intense than Dominik's or ever Somchai had in intense situations. Randy was shocked at this sudden expression, while, staring at Sarah, Akira still held the katana against Reus. Reus was shaken internally with the expressions expressing that clearly. He swallowed heavily. His ideology turned back onto him in a matter of seconds. His expression faded under his mask at the exclaim.

The surroundings were quiet, as death, again for another half minute.

The wind seemed to have stopped while it still interfered.

Sismo stood with more confidence again.

"*T-That* was important..."

"HOW?!" Sarah yelled even louder.

"D-Dont you understand the poor animal lived in dismay?" Reus couldn't answer. He couldn't even look straight at them. Couldn't even put an eye on them through his dark glasses due to the war of realization feelings in his mind.

Dom pulls the trigger again.

"Hold it." Said Sarah with full authority, covering the upper portion of the gun body with her hand.

"Shouldn't we just finish it already? You know how I am. Never wasting time..." Dom replied with disdain.

A whistle rose into the silence followed by loud barkings. The wolves were active again!

The only human the wolves didn't leap for at that time was Reus. *Could Reus control these animals?!*

Randy shot a bullet in the air to scare the wolves away as a sign of action. Both at the same time.

"Akira! No time to fight! Run!!" Randy yelled from a distance to Akira, holding the katana to fight. She turned to run as well.

<u>*S.I.S.M.O. clause A33*</u>- *If it's important, run, even if you've lost your arms and legs.*

'You can't move me with your words to convince me that you're right! You clever-clever Sismos... I know words are your secret weapon just like the famous saying!' Reus thought. "Eat them alive!" The order to the wolves.

The speed drastically increased of all the Sismos while they were not in a tactic for a retreat this time.

That would be useless with the current situation.

Running away while they still can was the only and the best option, otherwise, they would not live to see the unforeseen future with their eyes but rather would be skinned by the wolves and eaten to the core by some other scavengers in the next twelve hours or so.

Animal hunting is strictly prohibited and referred to as one of the most hideous deeds a Sismo of only a twisted man could ever do.

Twisted minds always end in the sismo prison.

The passage they followed, with all the cold wind that was touching their faces, felt like running through the dark, scary, cold woods as they show in some thriller 3D movie. Jumping, passing, leaving all the past winds behind while a beast chases you. Running at full speed as if they were flying.

The entrance became much bigger as it came closer and in no time they were into and under the open skies light again with a luminous beautiful aurora shining above them. But the race hasn't stopped yet. The chaise game of the wolves was still on the go!

'_Can't believe, we... We did make it..!_' Dom thought to himself while his heart was racing like crazy. It is said that human real capabilities only activate when in a survival situation. It felt so true in real time! _Surpassing the wolf speed!_ All of them were panting heavily. And with the heavy clothes, they were wearing, running was an even harder task. But there is no choice and they proved really good at it!

But Randy's leg slipped with a log and his face fell straight to the ground. The wolves immediately leaped straight for their prey! They started biting him. Randy tried to save himself but before the hungry pack of wolves, he was disempowered. The best? He could only try a vain practice to save himself while he still could before finding out that his body was eaten up by them.

He was still struggling harder and harder, yelling to gather some strength against them. The only default defense that he occupies is hidden beneath the heavy clothes he was in which the fangs of the wolves were unable to pierce through but couldn't say how long would last.

"Sarah..!" Yelled Akira as Sarah jumped straight into the wolves' pact to save Randy. Tears of terror fell down from Akira's eyes. The wolve's pack immediately concentrated upon both of them as Sarah submerged in their population. Dominik shot his last bullet in the air. That saved some space for both Sarah and Randy as the wolves leaped backward with fear due to the loud noise. Sarah was sitting upon Randy while Randy himself was lying on his left on the snow floor. She was still fighting while Randy was half-conscious. Their skin and clothes were salvaged or scrapped.

They were looking badly injured while, still, Sarah was gritting her teeth with a rageous expression on her face, revealing that she still had a life to fight. The wolves leaped for them again and in no time they were again attacking their midnight feasts.

"Hold back your katana-" Dom said to Akira looking at the haphazard situation.

"Why!?" Akira yelled back at him with a cry, melancholy on her face while her katana still faced forward in her hands.

With the same whistle as heard earlier inside the woods, the wolves returned, leaving their prey behind on the ground and Reus came out nonchalantly from the same entrance with his hands in his pockets. They wondered again if he was a bit underdressed for the cold. But that was a useless thought.

It was the entry of the ultimate **antagonist** of the story out of the dark forest.

"Привет Сара. Прекрасная ночь, не так ли? (Hello Sarah. Marvelous night, isn't it?)" He said in his intimidating, sexy voice again. "Новый парень, на котором ты сидишь, мертв? Не похоже... Я мог наблюдать, как его ребра расширяются и сужаются. (Is the new face you're sitting upon dead? It doesn't seem so... I could observe his ribs expanding and contracting.)" Randy's face was covered in thick dripping blood and already looked like a dead body. Save that his eyes were stifled open and he could still see and analyze what was happening around him. "But he looks almost dead meat. But I'll soon throw you to them for the words you said to me! (His voice was rather more grave this time) Oh! Sorry (He said with s stifled laugh) I forgot you can't understand that..." He passed a short laugh lifting his view from her to Dom and Akira above.

Sarah understood all that he said but she didn't feel like passing a single word as a reply to him, only expressing her stern expression. That was Sarah when she hated someone with her heart and was already killing a person in her mind.

"The wolves won't return don't worry... I quite have a sense of value for saving the lives of poor animals and humans you know? Who knows if you might kill all of their population for your own safety... I mean, I am not like those bigoted, mindless, nutty, trivial, and off-the-wall types.. how could I address you further, huh? Oh yes, a SISMO! With Sismo I remember but I do kill useless animals that are harmful to others! If he isn't dead already then I shall take the responsibility." With the word, he revealed his shiny metal chain from inside his big coat tied with a long, blunt hook-shaped knife, a *Kusarigama!*

'F-fucken asshole...' Randy's expression didn't change at all. He still looked dead.

"これはまずい...いや...！(T-This is bad... No..!)" Akira yelled and ran forward to save Randy and Sarah!

'That's not my style of fighting, it's more preciousness!' Sarah thought in the meantime. 'But I also know how to make use of this acquired heavy body because of clothing!!' Sarah battering rammed Reus before he could do something and because of her heavily clothed body he was pushed a few steps backward! But Sarah, affected by the wounds and because of the energy drained due to the furious fight, fell straight to the ground before him.

"Oh, nice! I got a great push." He yelled with a sadistic smile. "Why Sismo girls are always so beautiful and rigid in fighting at the same time? Well, I like that proposal!"

ДАВАЙ ДРАТЬСЯ.
(LET'S FIGHT.)

TICNHMI
BULLET!?
ТАК У НИХ
ТОЖЕ есть
ПУЛИ!! Я-!
(SO THEY HAVE
GUNS!! I-!)
ZOOP...

I MIS-SED IT AGAIN !!!
WAIT—
WHO'RE THESE GUYS APPEARED BEHIND ME OUT OF NO WHERE?
AND HOW DID HE GET SO CLOSE TO ME IN NO TIME?!!
I CAN ATTACK BUT NOT THREE AT A TIME...
I AM AMBUSHED!
IS IT REAL?!
I-I AM DONE...
A-I CAN'T MOVE IT! WH-!
!!
NOW'S THE TIME!!!

SPLASH!
WITH MY TECHNIQUE I CAN CUT THROUGH SKIN AND EVEN CRACK BONES...
HOUYA!
!
GAZE~
YOU SISMO BITCH!
УКЛОН ЯИСЯ ЭТОПО!
DODGE THIS!
!!!
I AM SAVED!... HE'S TOO QUICK!

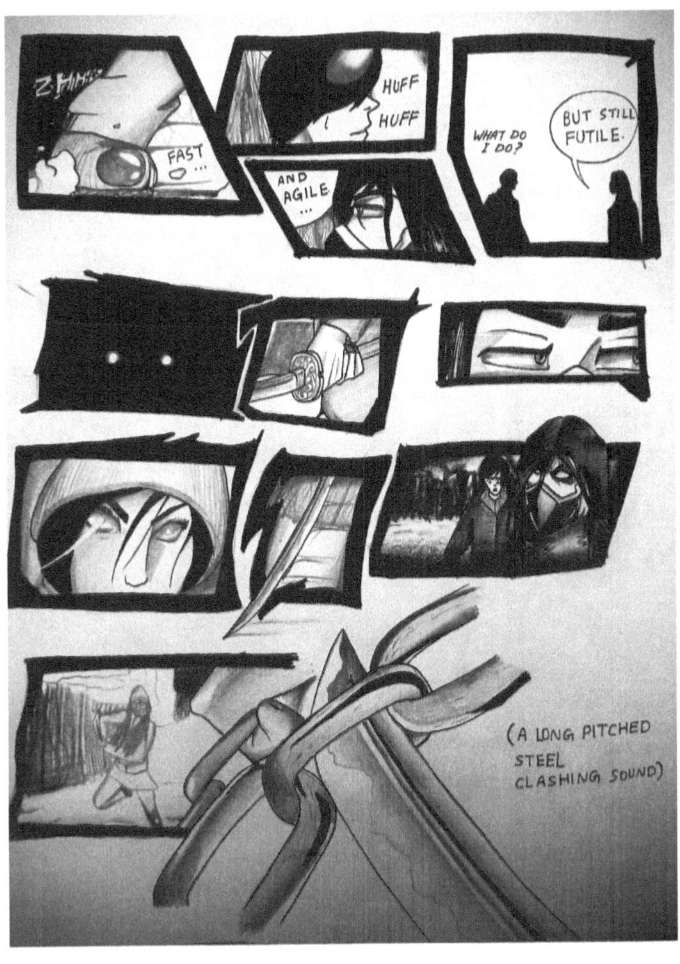

ZHINE
FAST ...
HUFF
HUFF
AND AGILE ...
WHAT DO I DO?
BUT STILL FUTILE.
(A LONG PITCHED STEEL CLASHING SOUND)

The fight went on for a long while and Reus fell to lose...

"Let's-" He fell straight like Randy did with a strike on his face!

"Idiot narcissist... We didn't hurt a single wolf," Dominik had thrown his empty gun to his face. His expression was so nonchalant like the situation was of no interest to him. It's, his expressions, mostly like that during his missions, and then he started playing with his hair above the left ear again. Gripping it with his thumb and rolling it around his left index.

Akira watched him with wide eyes as Reus was, in pain, twisting and turning his body vigorously on the snow ground with both his fists upon his face with drip lines of rich dark blood. She ran to see Randy who was smirking like a villain, seeing Reus getting beaten in such a manner and that they both were at the same level now.

He had gained consciousness again?

"Brother you okay?"

"Entirely..." His vision was still stuck upon Reus.

"And that my friends," Dom put his hands into his pockets from his hair. "Is called right in the bull's eye... Take him under custody! The case is closed."

'Tch... *Sir has so boasted of himself again.*'Thought Randy with a disdainful expression while Sarah helped Randy with her shoulder to walk home. His feet were still shaky after the wolf attack.

"Y-your,... dismissiveness..," Said Reus in pain to Dominik. "This is unforgivable..." He had still his eyes squeezed due to the impact.

"Crimson," started Dom down at Reus. "It's so beautiful." He continued staring at the blood on the ground and started on his smartphone with something.

Messaging...

"I see that you are getting really upset by my nature but that's how I am. The weather is getting extreme. There would be more SISMOs coming right away to arrest you. And you would be put into the *S.I.S.M.O. Prison.* Prey that they find you in one piece. Please don't hate me." He passed a hearty smile to Reus and turned back with his final words.

Those were his goodbye words *that bugged Reus even more...*

"Randy, with precaution..."

"Huh? Yeah..." Sarah's shoulders were heavied with Randy's right hand as he stood up and started to move. They abandoned Reus behind on the *crimson spot,* as Dom wrote in the message amid Reus still wailing slowly in pain between snowy white winds. The snow that the wind carried with itself started to rest upon his body while Sismos disappeared into the dark abyss in front of his squeezed eyes due to pain.

"More Sismos are on the way," Dominik started nonchalantly, facing forward. "They were the nearest one in this area so that was the best option to call them. Now, they'll arrest the cunning hunter for the *prison* once and for all."

Nobody replied saved they shared glances.

> *"One important thing was that Akira's confidence was shattered for some time when Reus blocked her Katana attacks. Save it was only for that one moment, she was trying so hard to burst out into tears because she saw it as her worst insult as a Sismo. She wasn't revealing her true current feelings yet that she experienced what is called broken."*

Akira was moving like she was so tired while Sarah was still half-carrying Randy to walk.

"Please call the Doc as well. The one who cured Hiroshi..." Akira said in her cute but low voice.

"I've already finished that part... All we need to care about now is (coughs)... is getting home safely. I can see that the mark of katana has become so obvious on your head."

"It's just a mark. Uh, do you need something?" Akira asked.

Dom showed her his left palm as a *'No thanks.'*

"No," Said Randy slowly.

"The weather's not good tonight. The weather's getting worse. We gotta go real quick!" Said Sarah with an intimidating expression again while her hair moved away from her face with the wind.

The wind suddenly started to make everything blur around them due to the increase in snow carriage. It more likely was a small snowstorm. But by the time a minute after they left Reus, there was a familiar eerie sound of some flying object. It was coming from far a distance and headed right towards them as they realized it. It sounds like some copter or chopper and is not alien to the ears. That was, without a doubt, a drone!

Some smoke of snow uncoveration made the sky clear and they saw blinking red-green lights in the air. Speeding towards the route they just passed.

"Wait," Making his mind still from the drone, Randy suddenly remembered something really important. "Sir,"

"Y-yeah!??" Everybody moved their face to Randy from the flying object in the sky.

"Randy, don't talk..." Said Akira with concern.

"Wait. Sir, did you bring the gun with you? T-that I gave you?"

"Wh-? No. It was important to throw it to keep everything in control. I thought it was empty so Reus couldn't use it as offensively as it is to its true potential."

"Empty... You mean you used all the *ten* bullets?"

"*Ten*?! No! Weren't there only six in it?"

"N-No, sir..! That was the agency pistol." Randy said after a pause. The wondering expression on his wounded face was much clearer. His face was filled with red bruises-on his forehead, right cheek, and right side of the chin plus a thousand cuts by the wolf's fangs and dripping blood were now visible as they focused on him with wide eyes.

They all were stunned for a moment and then suddenly there was a colossal blast behind them a few meters from a route they followed to go back.

Landmines?!

That was of so much impact with heavy bright light and sparkles with snow but the scariest part was that there was a painful cry from the source of the blast that sounded like someone's been burning in fire live and alive!

There was *no part of turning back!* They could see the yellow lights blooming from their house and it was in no more distance Sismos were headed in the direction of the implosion so they rushed in fear towards the house, filled their minds with fear and terror by the*impact of the shock wave!*

Fear was inevitable!

Meanwhile in the house;

"Shit!" Sylwia's connection with the drone was interrupted and then after a stuck screen, the screen went blank after a static. "Shit, shit, shit!!! What do I do now? They must be in danger! I saw the dubious with the gun..!" She was so restless and started to walk in a limited range in her room, covering the same path again and again, following the same path with concern reflected in her expression. "Hope they all be okay. Bóg(God), I am nervous..."

Real language strikes her due to nervousness.

After some time she went back to the remote screen and started to observe it in silence suffering a headache, her eyes straining and burning due to not having slept properly for days finally started to show its worse effect on her body. There was throbbing pain and a pulsing sensation in her head but she still ignored it.

Heavy bangs on the door came out of nowhere all of a sudden..! Sylwia jumped in her place and, with shaky legs, she walked towards the door and- "Who'se there..?" She asked.

CHAPTER FOUR

Later That Night:-

All the SISMOs were awake. Though she was injured, Sarah ordered everyone to shut tight all the openings of the house, (in case any of them were open or shut loosely) and to cover them with curtains as well. Dom caught a cold and Randy was covered with several critical wounds. Akira observed that all of them were in bad condition as she closed the door and moved back to them. Sylwia was prone to getting a migraine. While drinking water, Dom narrated the event that happened some time ago. He was still panting and Randy lying on the couch with blood stains that already looked to have dried with an even darker red shade. Sarah was also looking like a defeated warrior sitting on the couch while Dom was in his broodings that he missed the culprit being, as it seemed, their team's head the night. Solacing himself that it was indeed a norm in the rules to 'retreat if necessary(when you are unaware or futile in the situation)'. Sylwia also confessed to using the drone to check on them when they took a lot of time to return. Hannah put a blanket on Dom and Somchai and Akira cleaned the wounds with disinfectant and bandaged the wounds of Sarah and Randy as first aid.

The doctor was already scheduled for the next day.

Was Hannah upset for waking up so early as 5:00 in the cold morning?

Or was Dominik still more concerned about his beloved drone than the case?

And was Somchai upset too for leaving his imaginary girlfriend on his date in his dream for the case??

The doctor arrived at 8:00 in the morning and further checked and aided all those who were up for the mission late last night."

"One thing to remember is that she was the city doctor born in the same village where Sarah's house existed and was like the daughter of the villagers."

22 December 2022

9:00 AM

The sun rose after a long time in Greenland. Everybody was drinking coffee in the sun-lit house after a heavy breakfast made by Somchai, Akira, and Sylwia in the morning. Today the weather was warmer and some of the members were also sitting by the window to feel the sun and exploit the chance to the fullest.

"That doctor seemed so homie." Said Somchai with a blush sitting on the breakfast table.

"She's born in our village and we all know her. She studied in Nuuk," Sarah said rubbing her affected arm under the bandage.

"Nuuk? Some degree I guess." Somchai puts the coffee cup on the table.

"It's a big city. For Scandinavians, the authorization is easily transferable."

"ああ、助かったああ、助かった(Thank god)," Said Akira in an innocent tone turning back to the couch from her chair. "Randy... The *docotor* arrived or else you shall had became wild like those dogs."

"They're wolves, idiot..." Randy stared at her intimidatingly giving her chills and she turned her head back.

"Though he's hurt," Started Sarah. "Randy was lucky that I was there to save him when he was in that great danger. Otherwise, who knows what could have happened...(She puts the spoon down looking at someone in the living room near the TV). Doctor Onji, Vær venligst hos os i dag(Doctor Onji, Please stay with us for today's night)."

"Selvfølgelig, kære Sarah(Sure, dear Sarah)." Replied Doctor Onji with a smile.

12:00 PM

8 and Vaishnai were to arrive today and they were on the way-

"बोहोत दनि बाद हन्नाह और डोमनिकि से मलिंगे...(Will meet Hannah and Dominik after a long time...)" 8 said like chanting a lullaby and with a sunny-nosed face with an utter smile on his face.

"हाँ तुम सही हो लडक़ो! (Yes you are right boy!)" Replied Vaishnavi to 8 but in an informal manner.

"मैं बहुत खुश हूँ! (I am so happy!)" Said 8.

'Akira!'♥? He thought in his mind happily. 8 has a crush on Akira.

Shreyance Mani (or 8) insisted on joining in with them since he also wanted to join them in their mission and help them, unfortunately, it was too dangerous that they had to return.

Sadly, they had to leave when they knew about the degree of danger because of which they were sent to the lodge in the first place. That made quite an image in their minds that they were having a serious time in making everything normal again. They returned by the same Rolls Royce Cullinan. (Isn't it exciting how they were able to transport such heavy vehicles with them from country to country?!!)

However, they kept Paige with them for extra protection and support, their bodyguard, just the one like Randy.

"Surveillance," stated Hannah. "I think I look at it as our priorities."

"She's right," remarked Somchai. "We can't keep up with the plan any longer that we just came up with yesterday."

"Why is it, Somchai?" Asker Hiroshi lying on the sofa. "He's probably much weaker now and almost the same as before."

"With what happened yesterday, while it might be, he has a gun. And he can control animals as well(well it is supposed to). We can't cope like that. It's impossible! Plus, avoiding falling asleep is inevitable too. If it has to come then not even the will, even focus won't work..."

"But we have our night owls..." Says Hannah.

"Hey," started Sylwia. "Don't say that. Even we can't wake up for the whole night..! Plus, we are not some **owls**!"

"She's right," Sarah agreed too. "Don't address us like that. Plus, we are having a serious talk right now." She was much calmer than Sylwia.

"..." There spread a pin drop of silence as Dominik talked.

"He isn't so clever as well. He spends most of his time of the day just thinking about the sassy looks he has ." Dominik said.

"But what if he's been changed?!" Randy said. "He didn't seem the same as we used to imagine him from the last meeting."

"Indeed he's changed, not a lot but to a considerable form."

"We should call the *coil* and ask for assistance and devices," Sarah suggested.

"But Sarah," Hiroshi said in the middle. "We aren't even aware if we have its branch in here, *Greenland*!"

"Ma'am," Started Paige at Sarah while stroking Randy's wounded shoulder. "If I have permission to say, then I'd like to add that while we were coming to see you we were guided in all the ways possible to keep our security. Maybe we can just ask for more Sismos from the coil as I did."

Everyone's eyes widened as they were so glad by listening that they had not thought of it in a while.

"Yeah!" Somchai yelled with happiness.

"I almost forgot that!" Hannah said as well.

"Well, now we can start with a new design(plan) then." Said Dominik with a mild smile and folded his hands while moving his eyes to all the happy members. "We must first get our weapons. Jumbo please write an email to the coil. (Jumbo raised a thumbs up at him) Great now-" But just at that moment, there were knocks on the main door in the form of small taps. Sarah gazed at everyone and they shared a concerned glance, rather a confused one. Who was there **right now?** Who was this person to brake their conversation at this time of the day? When everybody was deliberately absent from the village...

After exchanging glances, Sarah walked slowly towards the door with caution. **Small cautious steps.** Since she was taking so much time there were several more knocks followed by a voice saying- "Isn't anybody home yet? I am at the door..." They released a sign of relief and Sarah opened the door with a mild smile. On opening, they saw that Judo was holding something in his big palm and constantly looking at it, and then he moved his eyes up. He looked so concerned about the thing.

"What took you so long?"

"That was nothing, come in."

"Hmm. Well, (removing his muffler) I found this in the doorway. The letter, *o-or whatever I should express it with,* was stabbed on the door pane, uh, sorry, bottom rail with a broken knife." He handed Sarah the same letter envelope that was puffed in the shape of something that was forced inside it. Some hard, cuboidal-shaped heavy kind of an object. The envelope was stretched out at all four edges of the existing heavy object inside and it looked like it would just be on the edge of tearing the envelope up. It was, the envelope, in fact, was burnt a little on one of its faces!

'Whatis *this weird?!'*

"Dom you're hurt?" Asked Judo.

"What is this thing brother and again, where did you find it?!!"

"Like I already told you; I found it stabbed it with a broken knife on the door and 'no'. I can't imagine what this creepy thing is. The burn is giving me the creeps... Oh, everyone's at the table I see!"

Sarah took the envelope with her and put it on the same table they were having breakfast on.

"What *is* this thing?" Dominik folds his hands.

'I already told you...' Thought Judo but didn't express through his expressions.

"Pass it here," Somchai took the envelope and cautiously opened it. Since it was unnamed they couldn't trust it. "As the leader, I must do this service."

"You're the leader?" Dom asks as if he is the leader himself with a smile. Som exchanged glances with his with a stopped hand for a second and passed a similar expression on the joke.

"Most probably this is Reus."Said Hannah.This might be but seems the not-quiet idea was somewhere on the back of everybody's mind. And *wallah!*; it certainly was him.

'То, как вы работаете, заставляет меня смеяться. Ваш стиль работы ужасен и смехотворен... Во всяком случае, переходя непосредственно к делу: «Встретимся прямо на северной стороне леса». Тот самый лес, в котором мы вчера вечером встречали СИСМО. И я дам тебе подарок взамен того, что ты подарил мне вчера на моем лице.!! Balsam fir...'

The way you guys work makes me laugh. Your working style is horrible and laughable... Anyway, coming directly to the point, 'Meet me directly on the northern side of the forest.' The same forest in which we met last night SISMOs. And I will give you a gift for the one you gave me on the face yesterday.!! Balsam fir(tree breed).

"*The letter was written in a very classy and beautiful handwriting. Probably Reus is showing off the whole of his classiness.***"**

"何?(What?)" Asks Akira.

"What the hell's written! This must be that damn Reus!" Randy was enraged in a second.

"Randy..! This is a duty hour..." Dominik said in a long word and stared at Randy's face with intimidating eyes.

"Sorry, sir..!" Randy, as a bodyguard, replied in an attention pose.

"This is Reus," declared Somchai. "He's calling you guys to meet him directly at the place you met him yesterday. The same Balsam fir forest that we could see in the distance." Somchai and Dominik are the only two there who can understand Russian.

"Balsa- What?" Akira started. "So that forest isn't the Greenland mountain ash?"

"NO, it isn't," Sarah replied. "Who told you so?"

"Oh... *My research was wrong then...*"

"No matter what," Started Hiroshi with full energy. "He'll not be missed this time and we'll then continue what we came here for! Jumbo are you finished?"

"Yeah, I've finished the part of writing the email and they are confirming it to be delivered by tomorrow through the **super express.**"

"そうすればライオンとも戦えるよ！(Then we'll be able to kill a lion as well!)" Akira says with enthuasiasm.

"There aren't no lions here Akira," Sarah replies to the enthusiasm.

"No," Hiroshi broke their conversation. "I meant that Jumbo's eating like an animal."

"Hello, son? You can't say that to your father."

"Shut up fat- you have the appetite of an angry god."

"Hiroshi! No time for jokes."

"Fine," Hiroshi folded his hands. "I just wanted to light up the moods of yours." He murmured.

"You believe this is safe?"

"..." Dom remained silent again.

"He must be fooling around. Believe me, we must not go!" Said Hannah in between Dominik and Somchai's talks.

"But Hannah," Said Sarah. "What if he wanted to have a face-off this time?"

Hannah- Yeah but we have so much to hold on to that way. Plus we can't ensure if he really yearns for a fight this simply.

"Based on what we saw yesterday he might be a great risk," Somchai said gravely...

"That's clear-"

"Do we really need this conversation!?"

"Hey, why would you interrupt me!"

"Hey,-" Before becoming an argument between Sarah and Dominik there were a few light bangings at the door.

"That scared me," Said Hiroshi lying on the sofa. "Who is it?" Everyone was so quiet and Sarah again walked to the door slowly. Since there was no one in that small village right now was the scariest thing but the knocks were still there. With shivering hands, Sarah opens the door!

It was just like when Judo was at the door a while ago.
"It would be a good experience for me to work with you. Aren't you gonna welcome me in?" He said smiling as everybody wondered and looked at each other's faces. It was then they realized that the mission just had started.

And it was already time for the mission to take some dangerous turns.

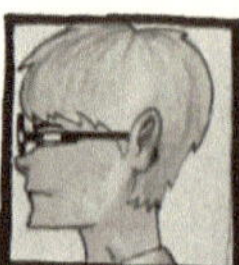

Hannah (Real name unknown)

Is happy, calm and kind to all. Gets easily irritated and angry just like his brother Dominik but on the contrary to his she knows how to deal with the strong emotions. A successful girl blogger and online seller.Expert in multiple weapons, both ancient (fans and ninjato) and the modern ones (ranged weapon).However. doesn't participate in most of the fightings. In her team she is among the four main members {Somchai, Dominik, Sarah and Hannah}
MONO CHROMATIC COLOR- White

Somchai McAdams

The leader of the EYES and the strongest in weaponry fights. Happy and cheerful with everyone. He may not look like but he has a heroic personality and respected by his comrades and also known as the "MASSACRE" among the other agents.

MONO CHROMATIC COLOR- Red

Dominik J. Santorski (Pet name)

Looks like any other anime character with dark hair. Clever and knows many forms of martial arts. The best leader in his team after his best friend the "massacre." An unruffled attitude for almost everything. Very creative at times but kinda lazy. His adamancy and nonchalant ness in fights seem so cool to observe!
MONO CHROMATIC COLOR- Blue

Yoshi Akira

Akira Yoshi, a unique member of the team in the sense that she still uses the traditional techniques to to defeat her enemies, inherited from her ancestors the SHOGUNS. She often acts childish and dumb but not at a mission. She learned advance fighting techniques with her katana and kunai.
MONO CHROMATIC colour-

Maroon

Judo

Standing at a height of 6'6 he is the tallest and physically the strongest by weight but lacks training and techniques by COIL because of less interest in missions. Mostly he doesn't take part in missions himself. Apart that he is blessed with a brilliant mind and is a good choice to take into the team that requires great planning for any mission as he best utilises their full potential.

Randy Warren

With fiery red hair that seems to match the intensity of his temper, the Santorski bodyguard commands attention wherever he goes thanks to the modelling career. His anger simmers just beneath the surface, ready to flare up at the slightest provocation. Piercing green eyes and freckles and nonchalance. He couldn't care less about the world around but the protection of his leaders, yet his presence is impossible to ignore. Best in hand to hand combat learnt from his past life and uses a simple gun as the weapon.
MONOCHROMATIC COLOR- Safery orange

End Of Sample

To be continued in the full version of this sample

'Greenland: Chronicles' Fall 2024-25:

WHAT YOU'LL GET?!

- Extended storyline! + Issaja's back story
- Character introductions!
- More mangas!
- Coloured pictures!
- Greenland: Sample rewritten (with better changes)!
- Would be available in both Paperback and Premium HARDCOVER!!

Fall- 2024-25

*(We'll try our best to publish the full version of this Anime novel **ASAP**)*

THANKS FOR READING AND BECOMING A PART OF THE S.I.S.M.O. FAMILY!

YOUR RESPONSE IS THE MOST PRECIOUS THING TO US RIGHT NOW AND WE WOULD LOVE TO HEAR FROM YOU!

RATE THIS PART OF THE BOOK (SAMPLE) ON THE WEBSITE YOU PURCHASED IT FROM. ALSO, TELL US WHAT YOUR FIRST

★☆PRECIOUS EXPERIENCE☆★

WAS LIKE WHILE READING OUR SAMPLE BOOK FOR THE FIRST TIME!

Don't Miss It!

<u>That Night by S.I.S.M.O.-#Firstknownmission</u>,a mysterious intruder enters the *Santorski Mansion* and is not planning something so good. He's dangerous, he's mad but, most importantly, he's a *SISMO HUNTER!* Only one of the members, who is a S.I.S.M.O. himself, is aware of his presence and plans to capture him alone about whom he came to know harshly! Check out the book to know what happens next...

S.I.S.M.O. SKETCH N' DRAWING BOOK- A promotional SKETCH N' DRAWING BOOK with an immersive design and wonderful big bright pages with the S.I.S.M.O.'s description inside!

S.I.S.M.O. is a secret group of people around the World.

"S.I.S.M.O. existed from the start of human civilization. Over the last three centuries, there have been many disappearances of criminals. At their retrieval, most of the criminals became completely changed men, who served society and helped in convincing everyone to follow ethical life and lived a more radiant life ever since. While those criminals who remained adamant about the training were never seen again. **Evil is better off dead.**

Don't you think so?

It is a secret group that only those who are the members know exactly about and any random individual can't tell if the person standing in front of him is a Sismo or not.

They are not like a terrorist group or dark web users, but rather 'agents' who are chosen from the public itself by other Sismos who believe that a particular man/woman chosen can be a new member of the Sismo group or community as well.

The people chosen as Sismo live normally like every other person, but he must hide his Sismo identity from everyone else(since it can only be known to another Sismo.) And at times when they are called by the higher authority (whom they call 'BOSS'), they must retire from their work at the present and must report to the place allocated to them by those higher authorities on time, which is usually in cafes or parks or just by the roadsides or at any public place. This helps in keeping their identities personal and unnatural.

They are assigned different missions and based on the level or degree of danger and importance the members are selected based on their long years of training and brain-boosting to solve the matter while being fair to the government and Laws.

Sismos are among those secrets of the government that are kept hidden by them from the normal public, like alien sightings.

They are spread all over the World and work for the welfare of the people and especially they are so bound that they can't talk about being a sismo to family members. Their ways are different however, they might kill you too if they feel that you are just like a burden on society. But that's not so obvious. They'll try to make you an efficient and higher-valued person in any way possible. Hence their ways of thinking are different from normal people's as well.

But that doesn't mean they are bad people anyway. Rather right. Many hate them calling their deeds cruel murder but it's not like that.

All the characters presented to you are SISMOs themselves! And that's why we are defining the SISMOs for you.

Everything else about a SISMO group and its history (how it started) will be revealed in our new upcoming novel, DEAD BITE, available shortly. "

Stay tuned!

Follow our YouTube Channel for the latest updates; Become a member of our group/ family by subscribing!

@mutekinobuntai23YTbusiness

MUTEKI NO BUNTAI

無敵の分隊

Coming Soon.